The Protector

A Short Story

(Revised Edition)

The Protector

A Short Story

(Revised Edition)

Yolonda Tonette Sanders

Yo Productions LLC

Columbus, OH

ISBN 978-1-7368659-0-3

ISBN 978-1-7368659-1-0 (e-book)

Yo Productions LLC

7185 E. Main Street

Unit 1543

Reynoldsburg, OH 43068

www.yoproductions.net

Cover Design: David Sanders Jr.

For information regarding special discounts for bulk purchases, please contact Yo Productions at 614-452-4920 or info_4u@yoproductions.net.

Printed in the United States of America

Acknowledgments

Acknowledgments are not the easiest for me to write because I'm always concerned about forgetting to include someone. It's important to me for others to know that I do not take them for granted. Anyone who truly knows me knows how appreciative I am, so I guess I shouldn't be trippin' when it comes to this section. Clearly, I'm overthinking this right now. (I always do.) Note to self: relax, take a deep breath, and begin.

To my Heavenly Father, without You, there would be no me. Thank You for reminding me that I can do all things through Christ, and for walking with me every step of the way.

To my hubby, you are one of a kind. We are so different and yet we complement each other extremely well. I love you, I thank God for you, and without your support, I would not be able to do half the things that I do.

To my children (via birth and bonus), I know y'all are claiming to be all grown and stuff now, but you will forever be my babies. The blessing of having each of you forever changed me.

To my grandbabies, Khari & Khia (man, that makes me sound "old," but I'm not. Lol), your "Nini" is crazy about you. While you don't live near, know that you are always close in my heart. Dynasty, technically, you are my "niece," not my granbaby, but my heart can't tell. I love you, girl!

To my mom, I miss you, lady. I can't write too much more or I'll be in tears and never finish this section. Rest in peace, pretty lady. I will forever love and cherish memories of you in my heart.

To my dad, you are much appreciated. I admire the way you stay active and hope that we have many more years together.

I want to give a special shout-out in the memory of Obieray Rogers, who worked with me under her company (Rubio Publishing Consultants) to publish the first edition. Obie, I miss you! Rest in peace.

To Nick and my mother-in-law, Janice, thank you for also helping me with the first edition of the story.

To my family, friends, and others, I want to express my heartfelt gratitude, especially my brother, sister-cousins, and sister-friends. If I have neglected to mention anyone by name, please charge it to my head and not my heart.

To all readers, I hope you enjoy this short story and that it is a blessing to you.

Much Love and Many Blessings,

Yolonda Jonette Sanders

The Protector

Seven Years Ago . . .

Breathe, honey!" Niles encouraged his wife, Yvonne, as she lay on the birthing table clutching his hand, draining it of all blood and circulation.

"Push!" the doctor instructed.

Breathe. Push. Yvonne didn't know if she could do both simultaneously. The pain was excruciating, and it was too late to request an epidural. So much for wanting to do this the "natural" way. Now she wished she'd heeded the words of her grandmother. *"Girl, you're crazy! I wish epidurals were around when I gave birth."* Nana had been right! She *was* crazy, and her insanity had been confirmed that very moment!

As Niles and Dr. Panton continued their directions, Yvonne pushed and pushed and pushed some more until finally, she succeeded. The new mom had expended all her energy. Exhausted, she passed out.

When Yvonne came to, the room was quiet. She spotted Niles and Dr. Panton in the corner whispering. She looked around the room, disappointed that she didn't see the bassinet. During their birthing classes, they were encouraged to keep the baby in the nursery as much as possible. "You'll have plenty of nights to spend with the baby when he or she comes home. Some nights you are going to wish the baby could sleep elsewhere," the birthing coach had said.

While Yvonne hadn't yet been sold on the idea, she understood the logic behind it. Nevertheless, though her throat felt scratchy and dry, she conjured up enough energy to speak. "I want to see my baby."

Niles and Dr. Panton both rushed to her side. "How do you feel, honey?" Niles gently brushed hair out of her face.

"You gave us quite a scare," noted Dr. Panton. "I'm glad to see you're alert. Your vitals are strong." He looked at Niles. "I'm going to give you two time alone. Have one of the nurses page me when you're ready for me to come back." Dr. Panton patted her leg. His hand lingered for a moment as if he wanted to say something more. Instead, he patted her leg again. "Call me when you need me," he said to Niles who nodded. Dr. Panton then took a deep breath and walked away.

Yvonne looked at Niles. Something wasn't right. "Where's our baby?"

A tear made its way down one side of his cheek as he came closer to her. Yvonne found herself welling up with tears and taking several deep breaths. They had prayed for a healthy baby. Despite preeclampsia, gestational diabetes, and bed rest for the last nine weeks, they had made it to delivery. As Niles struggled to speak, Yvonne braced herself for the news of whatever imperfections their child would have. Mental disability, missing limb, Down's Syndrome . . . it didn't matter that their baby wasn't perfect. Their love was, and that was what counted most.

"Tell me," she urged. The quicker she knew the diagnosis, the sooner she could prepare.

"She, um . . ."

It's a girl! A slight smile formed. They had decided not to find out the baby's sex beforehand. Equipped with this new knowledge, Yvonne now had a name to associate with her child. "Isabella." She said the name for the first time with certainty now that she knew she'd given birth to a baby girl.

Niles nodded. "Yes, Isabella was seven pounds, three point five ounces." He blew out a deep breath. "Honey, I'm so sorry." Tears raced down both cheeks. Yvonne felt nervous. Niles wasn't a crier. "She . . . she didn't make it."

As her husband's words sunk in, Yvonne let out a gut-wrenching scream. The precious child they'd struggled to conceive was gone. Yvonne had not even gotten a chance to hold her.

Current Day

Aiden grinned from ear-to-ear as his parents and circle of friends sang *Happy Birthday* in honor of him reaching his fifth-year milestone. As Niles helped him blow out the candles, Yvonne looked on with admiration at her husband and son. After losing Isabella and then needing an emergency hysterectomy after giving birth, Yvonne never thought she'd experience the joy of motherhood. In fact, she wasn't sure to what extent she'd ever experience joy again. Shortly after her release from the hospital, Nana passed away. Yvonne was left with no other biological family members since she'd never known her father, and her drug-addicted mother had abandoned her long ago at the age of two. That happened over forty years ago, and Yvonne had never heard from or seen her biological mother again. She had no memory of her. Nana was all she'd had.

To go from losing a child and then to losing Nana in such a short amount of time sent Yvonne into a deep depression. Not only did she mourn the baby she lost, but she grieved over those she had no chance of ever having. Adding Nana's death on top of that had emotionally overwhelmed her.

"Look, Mommy! I have a mustache." Aiden turned to her as he smeared frosting on his upper lip.

"Oh, my," she feigned shock. "Daddy will have to teach you how to shave now."

Aiden burst out in laughter. Yvonne smiled adoringly at her five-year-old blessing. She and Niles adopted him just three months after his birth. Yvonne had never thought she could love a child who didn't come from her own womb like she had loved Isabella. Aiden proved her wrong.

* * *

"You should go, Miss Yvonne. You and Mr. Niles deserve this time. It's your fifteenth wedding anniversary," Leyla, Yvonne's assistant and Aiden's nanny, urged.

"I know, but —"

"'But' nothing. You know I'll take good care of Aiden," she declared, sitting across the desk from Yvonne as the two women shared lunch.

Niles and Yvonne owned a successful trucking company on the west side of Columbus, Ohio. Yvonne took care of all the administrative stuff from home while Niles had an office in the warehouse. Yvonne used to have one there, too, until they were blessed with Aiden. She transitioned to working from home, and shortly after, she and Niles hired Leyla as an extra hand.

"Well?" prompted Leyla, "Can I get an 'amen' or something?"

"Yes, you do take excellent care of Aiden."

"Then, what's the problem? Why don't you trust me to keep him while you go on your trip? You have no idea how lucky you are that your husband wants to whisk you away on a romantic excursion. Don't keep discouraging him. He might get tired of asking. That's what happened with my parents. My mom started putting everything and everyone else in front of my dad, and well, he found comfort in the arms of another."

Yvonne snickered. "You're my assistant, *not* my marriage counselor. Besides, Miss I-don't-have-a-man —"

"By choice, I might add."

"Whatever. The point is that Niles and I are not your parents. Please don't compare us to them."

Leyla chuckled. "Oooh, she strikes back, and with a vengeance."

Yvonne fought back her laughter. "Why don't I fire you?"

"Because you love me," Leyla said with a huge, exaggerated grin, forcing Yvonne 's laugh.

Yes, she did love Leyla. The girl had been a blessing to the Braxton household. She had been a considerable help with Aiden. Niles had been pressing Yvonne to go to Mexico for a weeklong anniversary celebration. She'd told him "no," but apparently, he'd enlisted help. They'd never so much as spent a night away from Aiden since bringing him home. To go to another country seemed absurd.

"It's not healthy to be so obsessive, you know?" Leyla said seriously. "I mean, no offense, but you call like ten times to check on Aiden whenever you leave the house."

"Excuse me for wanting to check on my son. What loving mother wouldn't want to know that her baby is okay? I didn't know calling home was a crime."

"Well, let the record reflect that your 'baby' has never gotten hurt on my watch. I wasn't the one on duty when he had to get stitches in his forehead after sliding down the stairs in the laundry basket."

Yvonne glared at her twenty-something-year-old assistant. For someone on the Braxton payroll, the girl had a lot of mouth.

"I'm just saying . . . you're so worried about something happening to him when he's not with you, but even when you're around, he still gets hurt."

"You're also proving my point," Yvonne snapped back. "No one keeps as close of an eye on a child than a mother. If those things happen while under my care and I *know* I watch him, imagine what could happen when he's not with me."

"Are you going to be with him his entire life? What happened to trusting God? You say all the time that you pray for God to watch over and protect Aiden, but you never give Him a chance to prove that He does because you're too scared to do anything that doesn't involve Aiden being at your hip. Fear of something happening to him has immobilized you, and it's unhealthy if I must say so myself, with all due respect, of course."

"But, of course," Yvonne replied sardonically.

Later, after Leyla had gone home and Aiden was asleep, Niles asked Yvonne about her day. Specifically, he asked if Leyla came by and what they did.

"I know you put her up to talking to me," accused Yvonne.

He pretended to be confused. "About what?"

"Don't try it, mister. I have been giving some thought to this whole Mexico thing."

"And?"

"I'll go."

"Yes!" Niles scooped her up and twirled her around. "Baby, we need this. *I* need this time away with you."

"I know," she admitted. "I'd hate to say 'no' and you leave me for one of the employees at the warehouse," she teased.

"If I were going to leave you, I promise it wouldn't be for anyone at the warehouse. I'd probably go for one of our neighbors instead."

She playfully hit him. "I can't believe you said that to me. Niles Lamar Braxton, you owe me an apology."

"I'm sorry that it took you so long to realize how incredibly awesome your husband is. He appreciates being married to you so much that he planned this trip in honor of the love that he has for you and none other. You, Mrs. Braxton, are the love of my life. I'm so sorry if you can't handle the unwavering commitment I have to you and the growing love I have for you each day. You will have to live with the fact that I am crazy in love with you. How's that for an apology?"

Yvonne smiled, leaning in to give him a brief kiss. "And you, Mr. Braxton, will have to live with the fact that I am crazy in love with you as well."

* * *

Thank You, Jesus, Yvonne thought as she lay underneath the umbrella on the sand next to Niles. Day five in Mexico and all had been fantastic despite the rocky beginning. She had so much anxiety about leaving Aiden that Niles practically had to carry her on to the plane. The first night was r-o-u-g-h! There had been nothing romantic about the screaming match she got into with Niles when he took and hid her cell phone. She cried, accused him of being controlling, and said a few choice words for which she later had to repent.

Eventually, Yvonne admitted to herself and Niles that she had been living in bondage over the fear of something happening to Aiden. Though she didn't like the extremes that Niles had gone to help her overcome her anxiety, it seemed like a necessary step in her journey of healing. That night, she cried to the point of sheer exhaustion. She grieved Isabella, her nana, and the loss of everything she felt in life, including her mother, not knowing her father, or having any other family with which to identify. Everything she'd been holding inside came rushing out at once like water finding its way through a cracked dam.

Once a day. That's what she and Niles had agreed upon regarding her calling to check on Aiden. Playing by the rules, Yvonne used her one phone call wisely, video chatting with Aiden right before he went to bed so she could get a recap of his day and say prayers with him. She didn't know how she felt about his world not falling apart without her. Each day Aiden reported having "fun." He hadn't cried one time over his parents' absence.

"It's good that he's not crying every time you call," Niles had pointed out. "We'd both be a nervous wreck."

True! If Aiden were boo-hooing every night, Yvonne would have had no problems hightailing it back to Ohio to comfort her son. She was proud of him and made sure to tell him how much of a "big boy" he was. Aiden always gave a wide smile, displaying his missing teeth.

Yvonne and Niles spent day six snorkeling and hanging out with another couple they had met on the beach. Later that night, Yvonne called home from her husband's cell phone, as she'd done on all the previous occasions.

She looked at Niles alarmed. "It went to voicemail."

"Maybe Leyla didn't hear the phone. Give it a few minutes and try again."

Yvonne did just that and tried calling the home phone and Leyla's cell phone multiple times, all with the same results—voicemail.

"Relax, honey. It's not the end of the world. Call back in the morning. It's a little later than you normally call. They are probably both asleep by now. Since you didn't get to talk with him tonight, you can call him twice tomorrow."

Niles tried to sound light, but Yvonne's heart felt heavy. "Give me my phone," she demanded.

He didn't object. Niles disappeared around the corner of their suite and moments later, had the phone in hand. "Baby, I'm sure everything is all right."

Ignoring him, Yvonne turned on her phone. She had a lot of missed messages, but none from Leyla. Yvonne tried calling from her phone. Still nothing. "Something isn't right, Niles."

"I'm sure there's a reasonable explanation for this."

Yvonne could tell by his deflated tone that he wasn't as confident as he tried to appear.

Just then, his cell phone rang. Yvonne snatched it up. "Hello."

"Hi, may I speak with Niles Braxton?"

"This is his wife. Who's calling?"

"This is Melissa from Security One Alarm Systems. We're showing a panic alert at your residence and wanted to inform you that the police are on their way."

* * *

The trip from Mexico back to Ohio was the longest ride of Yvonne's life. She and Niles rushed home to find it strung with yellow crime scene tape and the chalk outline of a body on their living room floor. There were no traces of Leyla or Aiden, but there was dried blood everywhere. A lot of it. The police said that when they'd arrived, the front door was wide open, and they found an unidentified woman dead on the floor. Yvonne showed them a picture of Leyla and received confirmation that she didn't match the description of the person they found. Whoever the woman was, she had been stabbed in the abdomen. They suspected she'd been the one who hit the panic button on the alarm.

"We are trying to figure out the woman's identity. We've also issued an Amber Alert for your son. Mr. and Mrs. Braxton, we promise we'll do everything we can to find him."

Initially, Yvonne blamed Niles. He had talked her into going to Mexico, and now tragedy had struck. He took her accusations in stride, apologizing and trying to encourage her to pray. Later, she heard him crying in the bathroom.

"God, please, *please* let Aiden be okay," Niles wailed. The only time Yvonne had seen him shed a tear was after they'd lost Isabella. She refused to let her husband bear the burden of this by himself. If they had indeed lost Aiden, Yvonne couldn't bear to lose him, too. She walked in to find him leaning against the shower stall with his knees clutched to his chest. She sat next to him, putting her head on his shoulder, and they cried together.

* * *

Another day, another visit from the police. It had been four days in all since Aiden and Leyla had gone missing, and the same amount of time since Yvonne had a good night's sleep. The only thing that kept her sane during this time of uncertainty was prayer. She knew nothing of Aiden's fate, which troubled her immensely. It was creepy staying in a house where some stranger had been murdered, but Yvonne could not bring herself to leave. What if Aiden somehow found his way back home? They wouldn't know, and he would be traumatized to see the house empty, especially in its current condition. She and Niles had cleaned things as best as they could, but there was still more work to be done like ordering new carpet and repainting the walls. None of that mattered right now. Finding Aiden remained her only priority.

Yvonne also felt responsible on a deeper level. *You shall have no other gods before Me.* The words of Deuteronomy 5:7 convicted her. Motherhood had become her god. Deep down, she knew that she'd idolized her son. After such deep losses before him, when Aiden came into their lives, she'd stopped looking to God to heal her brokenness. Aiden became her panacea, and motherhood became her obsession. As much as she wanted to blame Niles for taking her away from him, Yvonne had to blame herself. Was God punishing her for putting Aiden before Him? Would Aiden suffer harm because of her? God wasn't like that. She reminded herself of Isaiah 55:8, *His thoughts are not my thoughts nor His ways my ways.* This was her opportunity to show God that she did trust Him. It became especially crucial to do so when the officers revealed some startling news to her and Niles.

"The good news is that none of the blood found matches that of your son or his caretaker. At this point, we have no reason to believe that either of them has been harmed."

"Praise God," Niles exclaimed, squeezing Yvonne's hand as reassurance.

Yvonne studied the officer for a moment. He looked pensive. "What are you not telling us?"

The officer sighed. "We have reason to believe that this is the identity of the young lady whose body we discovered." He put a picture before them of a dark-haired, heavyset beauty.

"Who is that?" Yvonne asked.

"This is Leyla Richardson. The *real* Leyla Richardson. Her family reported her missing the same night your caretaker and son disappeared."

"What are you saying?" demanded Niles.

"We're saying that the woman who has been taking care of your son for the last several years whom you know as Leyla Richardson is not her. We don't yet know the connection between the women, but we're looking into it."

"I don't understand!" Yvonne felt panic trying to consume her and swallowed it down. "We did a thorough background check on Leyla before hiring her. We do it for every employee. She came back clean."

"No, ma'am, Leyla Richardson came back clean. We've seen this kind of scam before. One person attends the interview using a false name. They then get the real person to do a drug test and pass the background check. Often people who are hard up for cash offer this service for a price. Leyla Richardson was a struggling single mom. I'm willing to bet that she sold her identity for a little extra cash. Leyla passed your background check, and then you hired this other woman who impersonated her."

Niles laid his head in his hands. "Can you tell us anything about Leyla, or whatever her name is, who has been caring for our son?"

"Not yet. I need to ask both of you a few questions. Start by telling me how this woman came into your lives."

* * *

In the days following, Yvonne and Niles learned that the woman they knew as Leyla Richardson was Carmen Dean, a former drug addict with a criminal past that included prostitution and theft. She was also Aiden's biological mother. She and Niles listened intently as the officer shared new revelations.

"We suspect that she waited years for the perfect opportunity to get her son back," the officer said.

Carmen's history revealed that before getting pregnant with Aiden, she had a four-year-old son killed by a former boyfriend who is currently serving time in the state penitentiary. Aiden's biological father was unknown. All they knew was that Carmen lived in a facility for unwed mothers until she gave birth and put Aiden up for adoption.

"Staff from the Hannah House have verified that Carmen used to be a resident there and gave birth to a son on the same date as Aiden was born."

"How did she know that we had Aiden?" inquired Niles. "It was a closed adoption."

"Only on your end. Remember, you folks had to go through a rigorous screening process. After which, the birth mother was given details about potential adoptees. Carmen was permitted to watch your tapes and learn more about you and the missus as people. The idea is to allow the mother to select the couple she feels will best care for her child. According to the staff at Hannah House, this helps put the moms' minds at ease about the adoption. Each mother can choose whether she wants the birth parents to have her information. Obviously, Carmen elected against that option."

Yvonne sat dumbfounded. Niles did all the talking. "Is this legal?"

"It's a rather gray area. I'm sure after this, Hannah House will rethink some things. They are lawyering up as we speak, afraid of the lawsuit you all may file."

"We don't care about a lawsuit. We only want our son!" yelled Niles.

"We're doing everything we can to find him. With the new information we've gathered, we don't have any reason to believe that Aiden is in imminent danger. Carmen is his mother."

"I'm his mother!" Yvonne fired back.

"Yes, ma'am, I'm sorry. All I meant is that it sounds as if she longed to be reunited with him. From your own admission, she took good care of him. Based on this, we don't speculate that she took him with intent to cause him harm but to care for him. It's not right," he quickly added. "I simply want to ease your mind that we don't foresee any physical harm coming to him."

"We don't care about your speculations," Niles said in an eerily calm manner. Yvonne knew that he was seething. "This Leyla, Carmen, or whatever her name is, has already shown that she's unfit to be a mother. Her first child was killed, the real Leyla Richardson has been murdered, and now she's taken off with our son without a trace. Don't tell me what you *think* she will or will not do. *Find her!*" he yelled.

The Braxtons had made it easy for Carmen to find them. Yvonne had placed an ad in the paper looking for a personal assistant. She and Carmen had clicked immediately. There weren't any indications that Carmen had ever abused drugs. According to the officer, Hannah House had helped her get and stay clean. The initial job posting didn't include anything about childcare. That role was added later when Carmen kept offering to help with different things concerning Aiden.

At the time, Yvonne was overwhelmed by both work and motherhood and appreciated the help. In retrospect, she had overlooked or justified some behaviors that should have caused her alarm. For instance, whenever Carmen was there, she took a greater interest in looking after Aiden than she did with the actual work Yvonne hired her to do. There were times when Aiden wanted attention so much that he distracted Yvonne from being productive. Carmen would tell Yvonne that she'd keep Aiden occupied while Yvonne got work done. Much of Yvonne's role required more than filing paperwork and making phone calls. Her responsibilities included taking care of payroll, keeping track of employees' leave, and making sure the company stayed current with all licenses and contracts. That wasn't the kind of work entrusted to an assistant, so Carmen's suggestions made sense at the time.

Yvonne could not deny that Carmen took excellent care of Aiden. Oftentimes Carmen went above and beyond the call of duty like the time Aiden had a fever of one hundred and three. Yvonne and Niles were both up with him all night on the phone with the doctor and responding to Carmen's repeated text messages. Eventually, Carmen came over to sit with them. It all made sense now. Carmen pressed for Yvonne and Niles to go to Mexico because she sought the perfect opportunity to take Aiden. Yvonne never let him out of her sight for long. The only way Carmen could get Aiden was if Yvonne was in another country. *Clever.*

Though she couldn't explain if asked, Yvonne was no longer frantic about Aiden's disappearance. Deep down, she knew everything would be okay. *When* it would be okay was another story. Hopefully, sooner rather than later. Her hope didn't rest in finding Aiden. It was in God whom she knew would work all things out in His perfect timing.

"Lord, I trust You," she said before drifting off to sleep that night.

* * *

Niles burst into the room, waking Yvonne from a deep sleep. "They found him! They found Aiden! Come on! We need to be down at the station within an hour."

Yvonne shot up out of bed and dressed in record time. She *thought* she showered, but she wasn't entirely sure what took place in the bathroom. Excitement ran through her bones. It had been twelve days since Aiden's disappearance. If Niles were right, the torture would be over soon.

Niles and Yvonne got to the station before the officers arrived with Aiden. They were taken to the office of the chief detective on the case, a burly man who looked like an NFL lineman.

"Mr. and Mrs. Braxton, I'm Detective Flowers. I hear my people have brought you good news. They will be returning your son to you."

"Can you shed some light on where they found him? Is Carmen with him? Is he okay? Is—"

"Mr. Niles, I understand your anxiety. I don't have all the answers, but I do know a few things. Aiden and Carmen were found in a hotel in Mason, Ohio, just shy of Cincinnati. One of the housekeepers found it suspicious that they had been staying in the room for over a week, but there were no suitcases or other items people normally bring when staying on extended trips. She said something to the manager, who looked up the file and saw that Carmen had used a Visa gift card registered under the name Yvonne Richardson to hold the room. Mrs. Braxton, she used your first name and the victim's last name."

"Yeah, I got that," Yvonne stated, blandly.

"Well, the manager heard about the news reports and started doing his own investigation. Long story short, the make and model of the car Carmen registered was the same except for the license plate. It turns out, our perp kept her car. Knowing her license plate would be flagged, every few days she would find a similar vehicle and swap plates. The hotel manager didn't know that, of course, but he did find the discrepancies between the plate she registered and the one on her car suspicious. He called the police and, well, the rest is history, as they say."

"How is Aiden?" Yvonne asked, irritated by the detective's narrative that included everything except what she wanted to know.

"He's fine. Officers said that he was playing a video game when they entered the room. Of course, he was a little scared, not knowing what was happening, but the overall report I received was that he's in good spirits."

There was a knock at the detective's door. "Come in."

When the door swung open, Yvonne's heart danced with glee. Aiden looked up and burst into a sprint. *"Mommy! Daddy!"*

Tears flowed from all their eyes as the three of them embraced. When they finally let up, Aiden spoke. "Why y'all stay gone on your trip so long?"

Yvonne laughed. "We're so sorry, sweetheart. We're back now, and we promise never to leave you again." She quickly thought about her words. Happy to have Aiden back in her arms, she didn't want to fall into the same unhealthy mindset that she'd had previously. "Well, we'll never leave you for that long again." Yvonne looked at Niles and winked.

* * *

As more details emerged about what happened between Carmen and the real Leyla Richardson, Yvonne discovered that Carmen had reacted out of fear rather than malice. Among other things, prosecutors charged her with kidnapping and murder, and her attorneys were aggressively working on her defense.

"She threatened to hurt Aiden," Carmen told Yvonne. Carmen had indeed paid Leyla to use her identity to gain employment with the Braxtons, but she claimed that she didn't have a plan to take Aiden away as the police had said. "I only wanted to be in his life and see him grow up." Somehow Leyla learned about Carmen's real connection with Aiden and tried to extort more money from her. "She came over that night and demanded that I pay her ten thousand dollars. At first, she said she would go to the police. I told her if she did, we'd both be in trouble. Then, she threatened to kidnap Aiden and keep him as ransom until I paid her. Miss Yvonne, I didn't mean to hurt her. She pushed me out of the way and started charging upstairs, and I did the only thing I could think to do at the time. I wanted to stop her from hurting him by any means possible."

"So, you killed her?" Yvonne tried to find the logic in Carmen's actions.

"That wasn't my intent. I only wanted to stop her from going after Aiden. Leyla was about twice my size. My strength alone wouldn't do it. After I stabbed her, she started screaming. I was afraid Aiden would wake up and come downstairs. I panicked. I ran to his room, put headphones on him to muffle Leyla's screams, carried him down the back stairwell, and we left. I'm sorry, I didn't know what to do. One child of mine already died because of my inability to protect him. I didn't want harm to come to another."

As tears swam down Carmen's cheeks, Yvonne could see the sincerity in her eyes. "When I went to Hannah House, I knew I had to get clean or I would destroy my life. When I read your profiles and saw the interview that you and Mr. Niles did, I knew that y'all would be great parents to my child. I honestly didn't mean to cause you any harm by working with you. I felt so lonely and only wanted to be close to Aiden. I love him. I loved him enough to remove myself from his life as his mother and give him a better chance with someone else."

"Why did you kidnap him? Why not go to the police?"

"I was scared."

Yvonne couldn't say whether Carmen's story was true about how things had gone down with Leyla, but she did believe two things—in her own twisted way, Carmen was scared, and she did love Aiden. While all the drama ensued around his disappearance, Aiden had been oblivious to the fact that anything had been wrong. He didn't see Leyla's body nor did he ever go without a meal. According to him, "Miss Leyla"—he didn't know her as Carmen—said that his "mommy and daddy were on a trip and might not be back for a long, long time." Because of this, Carmen told him that they were going to play an adventure game and go on their own trip.

The thing that warmed Yvonne's heart and prompted her to respond to Carmen's request for a visit was Aiden's report that "Miss Leyla said prayers wit' me ev'ry night, Mommy, like you do." A woman who kidnapped a child would not take the time to say prayers with him each night if she didn't love him in some way. More importantly, God loved Aiden so much that He protected him from experiencing fear or any of the other emotions that a child unlawfully taken from his parents would be subject to daily.

Yvonne wasn't crazy enough to believe that Aiden would never experience fear his entire life. Nor did she think that he would forever be ignorant of the dangers the world held. It didn't matter what was to come in the future. For now, she was thankful that Aiden's innocence had not been stolen. It had been preserved without being tainted. That could only be attributed to Divine intervention.

* * *

"Make sure Aiden finishes his math homework before being allowed to play his video game," Yvonne said to Angela, her new assistant and childcare provider.

"Yes, ma'am, I will."

Angela had come to them via referral. She was their pastor's daughter. She had no drug history, no other children, and no ex-boyfriend in jail for murder. She was a straight-A student at one of the local colleges and the leader of the young adult ministry at church. Still, they did a background check on her anyhow as was the protocol for all their employees.

"Bye, Mommy!" Aiden rushed her with a bear hug.

"Hey, li'l man, don't I get one, too?" complained Niles.

"Yes!"

After multiple hugs and "I love yous" were exchanged, Niles and Yvonne got in the car and left. The two of them were going to celebrate their seventeenth anniversary. It had been two years since the Mexico trip. Last year, they went away to the Caribbean Islands and rented a huge house, taking both Angela and Aiden with them. This year, the couple decided to go off alone to a hotel on the opposite side of town. *Baby steps.* The fact that Yvonne was leaving her son overnight at all after what happened with Carmen was a miracle.

Carmen had pleaded guilty to a whole slew of charges, including kidnapping and child endangerment, and was currently doing her time.

Occasionally, she sent letters asking about Aiden, and every now and then, Yvonne would reply with a brief update. Carmen promised that she would never interfere in their lives, but made no secret that she would love to be a part of Aiden's life in the future if Yvonne and Niles would be okay with it. Seeing how Carmen had some years to go before that would even be a possibility, neither Yvonne nor Niles felt any pressure to answer immediately. *Baby steps,* Yvonne again reminded herself. She'd been taking things one day at a time.

"You nervous?" Niles asked.

"A little, but I'm okay." Yvonne still dealt with anxiety from time to time.

"He's going to be fine."

"I know," she said. "God's got him . . . and so does Security One."

The couple laughed as Yvonne pulled up the video footage on her cell phone. It was an upgrade they both decided to get shortly after being reunited with Aiden. Yvonne smiled as Aiden sat at the kitchen table, doing his homework as she'd instructed.

Discussion Questions for The Protector

1. Put yourself in the hospital room with Yvonne and Niles. What are you feeling and why? What advice would you be able to share with the couple, if any?

2. How do you deal with grief? Are your techniques healthy or unhealthy? Please explain.

3. Yvonne reflects on Deuteronomy 5:7, *You shall have no other gods before Me*. Evaluate the areas of your life. Are there any places where you have made a "god" out of someone or something? Explain. What can you do to change things?

4. What part of this short story surprised you most? Why? What did you think would happen, but didn't? What did you see coming?

5. What lessons did Yvonne and Niles learn from their experience? What did you learn?

6. The front cover displays an image of a small child's hand in that of a larger male hand. What do you think the cover symbolizes and why?

Like *The Protector?* Scan the QR code to explore more books and products on www.yoproductions.net.

Connect with Yolonda online:

X: @ytsanders

Instagram: @ytsanders

YouTube: @YoProMedia

Facebook: facebook.com/yoproductions

About the Publisher

Yo Productions LLC was founded in 2008 by Essence® bestselling author Yolonda Tonette Sanders. The company's mission is to create, review, and publish works that S.H.I.N.E. — **S**timulate Minds, **H**onor God, **I**nspire Others, **N**ourish Hope, and **E**ncourage Growth.

As a **literary services** provider, Yo Productions specializes in proofreading, editing, ghostwriting, and consulting to address each client's unique needs. The company has offered creative writing workshops and hosted its signature Weekend Writeaway retreat to encourage relaxation and creativity among both established and aspiring authors.

As a **theatrical entertainment** provider, Yo Productions presents thought-provoking, dramatic performances that reach audiences from all walks of life. The company's motto, "Performance with Purpose," reflects its commitment to produce works with meaning beyond mere entertainment.

As a **publishing consultant,** Yo Productions guides authors through the complete publishing process, from manuscript to market-ready publication, including e-book design services. The company connects authors with print-on-demand distribution reaching over 40,000 retailers and libraries worldwide. Yo Productions provides expert formatting guidance and personalized support, treating every project like a bestseller.

To learn more or submit your work for consideration, visit www.yoproductions.net.

Please enjoy the following excerpt from *Soul matters* (20th Anniversary Revised Edition) by Yolonda Tonette Sanders.

Chapter One

The Perfect Package

It was ten minutes to three, and Wendy was eager to leave work on time. "Start cleaning up now," she said to her first-grade class. They had crayons, markers, and books all over the place. "Be sure to put everything back where it belongs. After you finish, line up at the door and wait until the bell rings."

Much to Wendy's surprise, her instructions were followed with little resistance. A few students mumbled about not being able to finish what they were doing. Still, even they cooperated without her saying anything else. Maybe they could sense that something was different about her. Toward the end of each day, the children usually had exploratory time and could choose between various activities such as reading, coloring, playing educational games, or anything else that Wendy deemed appropriate. She usually walked around the classroom and interacted with several students during that time. However, she sat at her desk like a watchdog this entire week, responding only when needed.

"Just a few more days . . ." Wendy murmured to herself. Next Wednesday, the school would be closed for Christmas break, and as much as she hated to admit it, she was looking forward to having some time off. Although only seven weeks pregnant, she was beginning to feel the effects of this pregnancy on her body. She used to have the vitality of a three-year-old, but lately, she felt like she would lose in a walking race against Methuselah. She was convinced that the term "morning sickness" was deceptive. If the feelings of nausea, vomiting, heartburn, and headaches were only confined to a few hours of the day, it would make the first trimester of her pregnancy much more bearable. Instead, she was liable to experience *morning* sickness at any given moment of the day.

While the children were cleaning up, Wendy was on the edge of her seat, waiting for the bell to ring. *Thank God it's Friday.* She didn't think she would be able to make it another day. She was going straight home after work. She would not leave the house until it was time to go to church on Sunday morning. After service, Wendy planned to go over to her parents' house to celebrate her father's birthday. Wendy hoped to feel better by next Friday when she and her husband, Kevin, were scheduled to go to Philadelphia and visit his family for the holidays. The Ohio native would rather spend her Christmas vacation recuperating from her ailments in the comfort of her own home, but there was no way she could back out of the trip now. Her mother-in-law was ecstatic about the pregnancy and could not wait until they got to Philly so she could show Wendy some of the things that she had already bought for the baby.

"Keep your hands to yourselves," she said to two boys who were shoving each other.

"He started it!" David stated, pointing at Jeffrey.

"Nuh-uh, he did!" Jeffrey pointed back at him.

"It doesn't matter who started it. Both of you knock it off," Wendy replied sternly. Secretly, she knew that David probably was at fault, but she didn't feel like investigating the issue. David was bigger than the other first graders in both height and weight. Jeffrey was one of those children who looked like he had been born premature, making him an easy target for David. Even though David was sometimes a bully, Wendy liked him, probably because he reminded her of herself.

Wendy had never been a bully, but she had been heavy and tall as a child. She used to feel awkward standing next to other children in her class. It irritated her when adults would ask how old she was and then say, "You look like you should be older than that." It wasn't until the summer before her freshman year of high school that she began to thin out. In her adult years, Wendy managed to remain a size eight, but she had to work hard at it, contrary to her younger sister, Kim, who naturally wore a size six.

When the bell rang, it was music to her ears. "Okay, let's go." Wendy jumped up and escorted her class to the pick-up area. Once there, another staff member stayed with them until their bus or a parent came to pick them up. When they reached their destination, Wendy said goodbye to her students and headed back to her classroom.

"Attention, all teachers and staff: Mrs. Phillips, please come to the office. Wendy Phillips to the front office, please," she heard Donna Burchett, the office secretary, announce over the PA system.

For what? Maybe I should go ahead and leave. No one would be able to say for sure that I was in the building during the announcement. Wendy was only a few doors away from her classroom, so all she had to do was grab her stuff and head home. However, she reluctantly turned around and walked toward the office at a medium pace. Her shoulder-length hair often bounced as she walked. Today, it was pulled back in a ponytail. Wendy hated ponytails and only wore her hair in that style when she worked out. However, since she had been experiencing morning sickness, she devoted less time to her appearance. She even had her glasses on, and Wendy normally wouldn't be caught dead in a pair of glasses.

"Wendy Phillips, please come to the office," Ms. Burchett repeated.

Coming! she wanted to yell. *I hope it is something simple like a signature needed on some paperwork that I filed.* She dreaded the possibility of a parent waiting to speak with her about a child's behavior.

"Hi, you paged me?" Wendy inquired as she burst through the door into the administrative office.

"Yes, dear, you had a telephone call," Ms. Burchett replied, exposing the gap between her stained teeth resulting from years of smoking.

"A telephone call? From whom?" Wendy asked, scrunching her eyebrows to indicate confusion. No one *ever calls me at work*. Her friends and family knew she taught and was unavailable during the day. "It must be from a parent. I'll take the message, but I'm not calling anyone back until Monday."

"No, honey, it wasn't from a parent. Someone called from Dr. Korva's office."

"Oh," she said nervously, trying hard to keep her composure and not panic.

"I wrote down the number." Ms. Burchett handed Wendy a piece of paper and pointed to the phone on her desk. "You can call from here if you'd like." She carefully studied Wendy's response.

"That's okay. I'll wait and call later since I'm getting ready to leave anyhow."

"The lady didn't tell me why she was calling, but it sounded important."

Wendy could tell that Ms. Burchett was fishing for information. Odds are, she had already tried to gather as much as she could from the person who called. Wendy hadn't told anyone at the school about her pregnancy yet, and now was not the time to make that announcement. "Thanks so much,

Ms. Burchett, but I'm sort of in a hurry, so I'll call back from my cell phone on my way home."

"Okay. I just hope everything is fine," she said with narrow, bluish-green eyes peering from the top of her glasses. "Are you sick, honey?"

"No, ma'am," Wendy said honestly. Her mind was so boggled with getting to a phone to return Dr. Korva's call that the feelings of morning sickness had been temporarily suppressed.

"Then why would someone from a doctor's office call you?"

As much as Wendy wanted to tell Ms. Burchett to mind her business, she couldn't. The woman was at least in her late fifties or early sixties, and Wendy couldn't strike up the nerve to tell her off. *If only I were a little more like Kim,* she thought, because her sister would not have wasted any time putting Ms. Burchett in her place. The two sisters had similar characteristics with dark brown hair, brown eyes, and dimples. However, Wendy's complexion was just a little lighter than Kim's, and she was also a few inches taller than her younger sibling. Both ladies favored their mother, but Kim had been blessed with a high metabolism and the ability to speak her mind audaciously. Wendy wasn't as outspoken. Besides, she generally liked Ms. Burchett, although this interrogation tested her patience. "I'm not sure, but I'd better run so I can find out, huh? You have a good weekend, Ms. Burchett," she said, backing toward the door.

"Okay, you too—and I'll talk to you on Monday."

Not if I can avoid it, you won't! Wendy walked out of the office and raced back to her classroom. She was so disturbed by the call that she rushed past several of her co-workers without speaking. *Why did Dr. Korva call me at work?* She didn't know, but she was desperate to find out.

When Wendy returned to her classroom, she grabbed the cell phone out of her purse only to discover a message waiting. That was nothing unusual because her phone stayed on vibrate during the day. A lot of times, Kim called her from the hair salon where she worked and left messages when she was between clients.

"Hi, Wendy, this is Susan, Dr. Korva's nurse. She would like you to come into the office today, if possible, to discuss your test results. She's leaving around four this afternoon. If you can't make it before she leaves, then you need to come sometime early next week. Please call the office and let the receptionist know what works best for you. The number here is 555-3794.

We hope to see you soon."

Wendy's heart sank. *Dr. Korva told me that they take blood and vaginal swabs to run tests on all expectant mothers. The only reason they would call was if something came back abnormal.*

She looked at her watch. The time was now three fifteen. It would be a stretch to make it from the southeast side of Columbus to the northern suburb where her gynecologist's office was located. Such a trip would take forty minutes this time of day, at the very least. Still, she tried to call the doctor's office anyway, hoping that, with any luck, they would squeeze her in.

Shaking and short of breath, Wendy wiped her sweaty palms on her clothing and dialed the number. "Hi, this is Wendy Phillips," she said, trying to hold back tears. "I'm returning a call to Dr. Korva. Will she be able to see me today? I can be there in about half an hour?" She altered her traveling time, hoping to increase her chance of being seen.

"Oh," she said solemnly when the receptionist said Dr. Korva was running behind schedule. Wendy couldn't be seen until Monday morning. "Well, can you tell her I'm on the line? Maybe she can just tell me the results over the phone." She crossed her fingers, praying that she would be transferred to the doctor. No such luck. Dr. Korva preferred to talk in person. "Okay, I'll be there at nine on Monday," she said, confirming the time of her appointment before hanging up the phone in despair.

How am I going to make it until then? She dreaded going back to the office and arranging for a substitute through Ms. Burchett. *Forget it. I'll just call in,* she opted. Sure, not submitting a request for a substitute beforehand was inconsiderate and unprofessional, but she didn't care at this point. Her main concern was finding some way to make it through the weekend without losing her mind.

Wendy got her stuff and headed for the car. She tried to talk herself into remaining calm, but it wasn't working. She felt lightheaded. *What if my baby has a mental disability? What if it's deformed or has some kind of genetic defect?* She tormented herself. She was afraid of what the doctor would say. She knew it was bad news. Her fear turned into anger toward Kevin. *I told him that his smoking could cause damage to the child, but he didn't believe me.* If Kevin just smoked cigarettes, she could probably deal with it a little better, but he sometimes smoked marijuana, and Wendy couldn't stand it.

Whenever she complained about his recreational activities, Kevin got upset. He would tell her that he was not doing anything that she wasn't aware of before they got married. True, Wendy knew about his smoking when they were dating, but it was different then. She was attracted to his street-but-sweet personality. She had never dated anyone so successful, yet a little rough around the edges. Plus, he was very pleasing to the naked eye. He reminded her of a Denzel Washington wrapped up in a Barry White voice. He was the perfect package: sexy, successful, and single.

Kevin's accomplishments intrigued her most of all. He worked hard for everything he owned and built his real estate business from the ground up. He was very successful and made well over six figures a year. He didn't have parents who could afford to pay for his education. He paid for it himself. He didn't grow up in the suburbs of some major city but lived in various ghettos of Philadelphia. His father left home when Kevin was only three, and his mother raised him, his older brother, and his sister with money she received from the federal government. He didn't let his life's circumstances prevent him from making something of himself, and Wendy respected that.

Foolishly, she convinced herself that Kevin would change the things that she didn't like about him once they married, but he hadn't. Now, nearly six months into the marriage, the honeymoon was over, and reality had settled in. *If something is wrong with the baby, I know it'll be all his fault*, Wendy told herself.

Please enjoy the following excerpt from *Connecting with Christ: 52 Weekly Devotionals to Nurture Spiritual Growth* edited by Yolonda Tonette Sanders.

Introduction

If you conduct an internet search for devotionals, I'm sure that you won't find a shortage of materials. The challenge when constructing this project was creating something different enough to draw others' attention without requiring an enormous amount of time. The goal is not for anyone to spend an exorbitant amount of time with this devotional. As wonderful as this project is, nothing should replace the written Word of God contained in the Holy Bible. My prayer is that this work leads you to *the* Word and enhances your understanding of Scripture.

Enclosed you will find 52 devotionals broken into 12 themes to correlate with the 12 months of the year. Although the devotionals are ordered, feel free to go through the themes in a manner that best suits your needs. There is only one devotional per week. Ideally, the hope is that you will read the devotional at the beginning of the week and meditate on the Scripture and overall message for the rest of the week. You are encouraged to read the entire passages of the Scriptures listed to see what the Lord may reveal to you outside of what is written in this book. There is a place for you to jot down your thoughts each week if you choose.

You will notice that this work contains no dates, only generic weekly references (e.g., week 1). This is so you can use the entire collection of devotionals for many years to come. You do not have to follow the order of the weeks or themes. Go through this book as the Lord best leads you. May you hear His voice loud and clear as you journey on this road called life.

Love and Blessings,

Yolonda Tonette Sanders

Renewal

renew = to make like new: restore to freshness, vigor, or perfection

Week 1: Renewal

External Wither, Internal Bloom
by Yolonda Tonette Sanders

Therefore we do not lose heart. Though outwardly we are wasting away, yet inwardly we are being renewed day by day.—2 Corinthians 4:16

Sometimes when I look in the mirror, I see a new wrinkle or mark on my body that wasn't there the previous day. And seriously, is that *another* gray hair! Reality hits. No matter how much water I drink, moisturizing cream I use, how healthy-*ish* I try to eat, or how often I exercise, it seems that my days of six-pack abs and cellulite-free thighs are likely long gone.

Face it, lady. You're getting old! I say to myself.

Getting old is one thing; feeling old is another. I don't lie to people about my age, and I still feel younger than what the calendar says I am. However, I cannot claim eternal youth considering that I have two adult children and two grandchildren. The fact of the matter is that I *am* aging, and one day this body of mine will eventually stop functioning altogether.

While my outer person is gradually weakening, the opposite is happening with my inner person. My faith is stronger than it was in 2001 when I first accepted Jesus as my Lord and Savior. My commitment to Christ is firm, and most importantly, my salvation is secure. I don't say that arrogantly but rather assuredly because I believe in the Word (John 3:16; Romans 10:9). Life has a way of wearing us down sometimes. However, the more I get to know God and experience His faithfulness during the ups and downs of life, the more I rely on and trust Him.

At various times in life, we stop to reflect on our past, present, and future. The new year is often one of those times as people make lists of resolutions, affirmations, and good intentions to be and do better. According to *Quartz*, the most common resolutions that people make relate to their physical health and finances. While there is nothing wrong with wanting to improve our physical health or to be better stewards of our finances, we must not be so focused on those things that we overlook the big picture—*everything* we see before us is temporary (2 Corinthians 4:18).

As sobering as the realities of aging may be or how important our finances are to our standard of living, those concerns should never outweigh our spiritual conditions. We should care more about how our hearts look to God than how our bodies and financial portfolios look to others. We can work on both our internal and external issues, but if we have to choose, internal is the most important (1 Timothy 4:8; 1 Corinthians 15:44).

The new year is often a time for a fresh start. Most of us have plans and goals, yet, we don't know if life will cooperate with what we have in mind. Sickness can wipe away good health. Situations like stock market crashes, unexpected job loss, and costly repairs can decimate finances, but no one can take eternal life from us (John 10:28–30).

As you think about what you want to accomplish this year, think about what you need *most*. During this time of renewal, start with your faith. The first step to spiritual renewal is daily submission to Christ. Each day, He will equip you with what you need for whatever lies ahead.

Father, I thank You for fresh starts. I am grateful that You do not hold my past against me, but You give me a chance to start anew. As I reflect on what I want to do this year and the areas in my life upon which I seek to improve, help me make my relationship with You the top priority. Renew me from the inside out, and help me remember that Heaven is my ultimate home.

*Information from Quartz comes from https://qz.com/1777619/the-most-popular-new-years-resolutions-and-how-to-keep-them/

www.ingramcontent.com/pod-product-compliance
Lightning Source LLC
Chambersburg PA
CBHW051829180726
48283CB00004BA/1361